A Real Home

Story by Marcie Aboff

Illustrations by Wendy Rasmussen

Chapter 1

Flory and her mom drove off the busy highway and onto the tree-lined streets of Hillsdale. Flory turned to look out the car's rear window. The long yellow moving truck was still following right behind them.

It was only a few more blocks until they turned the corner to Joe's street. Flory saw Joe and his six-year-old son, Nicky, standing outside their blue house. They both waved as Flory's mom parked her car.

Joe opened the car door for Flory's mom. He bent down and gave her a kiss. When Flory got out of the car, Nicky handed her a plush stuffed bear.

"Welcome home!" Joe and Nicky called out at the same time.

Flory tried to smile as best she could, but she missed her "real" home already. She had lived in Bay City her whole life. She liked it there. Her best friend, Jenny, lived there. She and Jenny lived in the same apartment building and were in the same grade. They had even attended the same dance class together ever since preschool.

A few months ago, when Flory's mom told her that she and Joe were getting married, Flory was happy for her mom. She liked Joe. He was nice and friendly, and his son, Nicky, was cute—for a little first grader, anyway. But when her mom told her they were moving to Joe's house after the wedding, Flory felt an awful pit in the middle of her stomach.

"Joe's house is much bigger than our apartment," her mom had said, trying to make Flory feel better. "You'll have a bigger bedroom and a real backyard. You can invite Jenny and the rest of your friends over as much as you want."

Flory still didn't want to move.

Flory watched the long moving truck pull along the curb in front of Joe's house.

Joe looked at Flory and gave her a big smile. "We have a surprise for you upstairs," he said. Joe and her mom winked at each other. Nicky jumped up and down. "Wait till you see!" he squealed.

What could it be? Flory wondered, suddenly feeling very excited. She hurried inside Joe's house and ran up the stairs. Her mom, Joe, and Nicky followed her.

Upstairs, Flory saw the bedroom door was closed. Joe walked up to the door and slowly opened it.

Flory's eyes bulged wide as she stared inside her new bedroom. Everything was pink! The walls were painted a light pastel pink, and the new carpeting was a deep shade of rosy pink. Even the blanket and matching curtains were bright pink with purple and green flowers.

Her mom beamed. "Surprise!" she said. "Isn't your new bedroom beautiful?"

Joe put his hand on Flory's shoulder. "I just finished painting it for you yesterday," he said proudly.

Flory said nothing. Then she frowned. She looked at her mother and said, "Mom, I HATE pink!"

Her mother's face look shocked. "Since when, Florinda?" her mother asked. "I thought pink was your favorite color."

"Not since last year when I was in second grade," said Flory. "My favorite color is blue now."

Chapter 2

Flory's mom covered her mouth and put her head down. Joe put his arm around her. Flory heard footsteps and noticed the moving men walking toward them. They wanted to know where to put the furniture.

"We better go downstairs and show them," said Flory's mom. Joe and Flory's mom walked back downstairs with the moving men.

Flory stared at the baby pink walls in her new bedroom. *How am I going to live in this room?* she wondered.

Nicky looked up at Flory. "I hate pink, too," he said. Nicky's room was blue, green, and yellow with a border of soccer balls that matched his blanket.

Flory looked at Nicky and sighed. "I guess we should go downstairs and help unpack," she said.

"OK," said Nicky cheerfully.

When the movers left, there were boxes piled all over the house. Some were empty and some still had tape on them and needed to be unpacked.

"I think we've all put in a full day of work. Let's get this family some food," said Joe. "How about pizza?" Everyone agreed that was a good idea.

They ate the pizza in the backyard. It was a warm night for the first week of September. In a few days, Flory would be starting her new school. She wished she felt excited, but she didn't. She felt a little nervous.

"There's a girl down the street who is the same age as you," Joe said to Flory. "Her name is Gail. She's on vacation this week, but I know she'll be at the same bus stop as you."

Flory nodded. Flory always walked to school in the city with her friends Jenny and Tamara. She never rode a school bus before.

After they finished eating their pizza, Flory went upstairs to put some of her things away in her much-too-pink bedroom.

Chapter 3

Nicky had his first soccer game on Saturday. Flory, her mom, and Joe went to see him play.

Nicky was a very good soccer player. He kicked the ball straight and hard. "Go, Nicky!" Flory's mom yelled as he ran to the ball. Nicky stopped the ball with his foot. Bam! He kicked it hard, right into the net.

Flory, her mom, and Joe all cheered. The other parents did, too. "You've got a future soccer star there, Joe," one of the other dads said.

Joe laughed. "Oh, yes, Nicky loves soccer." Joe introduced Flory's mom to the other soccer dad. Then he pointed to Flory. "And this young lady is my new daughter, Flory," he said.

Flory smiled and said hello. It felt funny having Joe call her his "daughter." Flory already had a dad—her real dad. She was looking forward to seeing him next weekend.

By the end of the game, Nicky had scored three goals. "Great job, Nicky," Flory said.

"Thanks!" Nicky said. "Will you play with me some more when we get home?"

"Sure," Flory said. She actually liked being the "big sister."

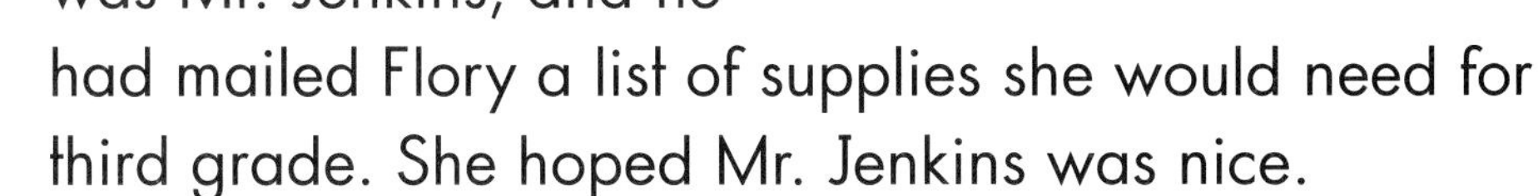

The next day, Flory went shopping with her mom for school supplies. She was glad her mom took off some time from work at the department store. Flory's teacher's name was Mr. Jenkins, and he had mailed Flory a list of supplies she would need for third grade. She hoped Mr. Jenkins was nice.

There were a lot of people at the mall. Flory bought a new backpack. It was blue and yellow. Her mom also let her buy some more school clothes.

Flory's mom looked at her watch. "We better go. I want to cook dinner tonight, and Joe likes to eat around six o'clock," she said.

"But that's so early mom. We usually don't eat dinner until seven o'clock," said Flory.

"I know, but Joe likes to eat earlier," explained Flory's mom. "Since I'm off today, I figured I'll cook dinner. Some nights I'll be working late and Joe will make dinner. We're working out a new schedule."

Flory wasn't happy with this new schedule. Her favorite television show was on at six o'clock.

Chapter 4

It was the first day of school. Flory picked out her clothes the night before. Her mom helped braid her hair into two braids the way she liked it.

"You know, this bedroom is really pretty," said her mom, looking around. "Are you getting used to it a little more?"

Flory shook her head no.

"All right. I'll talk to Joe about it," Flory's mom said. "I have to go to an early morning meeting before the store opens up. Joe is going to take you and Nicky to the bus stop. I'll be here when you get home from school."

Flory's mom kissed Flory goodbye. "Have a good day at your new school," she said.

Flory kissed her mom back. "Have a good day at work," Flory answered.

Flory grabbed her new backpack and walked with Joe and Nicky to the bus stop. "I hope it's not the same bus driver as last year," Nicky said. "He was always singing."

Joe grinned. "And what's wrong with singing?" he asked. Joe started to sing the ABC song—loudly. Nicky laughed, but Flory put her head down. She hadn't sung that song since kindergarten! Embarrassed, she walked a little ahead.

There was already a group of kids at the bus stop when Flory got there. Joe said hello to Gail, and he introduced Flory. "Hi, Gail, this is my new daughter, Flory. This is her first day at Hillsdale School."

"Hi!" Gail said with a friendly smile.

"Can Flory sit next to you on the bus?" asked Joe.

Flory winced. It was one thing to introduce her, but he didn't have to ask Gail to sit next to her!

But Gail smiled. "Sure, she could sit next to me," she said.

Gail and Flory sat in the middle of the bus. Gail was very friendly. She started talking about the different classes in school. Then she told Flory about the food in the cafeteria. Tuesday is pizza day and Thursday is hot dog day, but don't eat the macaroni and cheese on Wednesday—it's gross.

A few stops later, another girl came on the bus. Gail waved wildly to her. "Hi, Denise!" Gail called to the front of the bus. The other girl hurried back to Gail. But then she stared at Flory.

Gail pointed to Flory. "This is Flory," Gail said. "She just moved here."

"Hi," Denise said. Then she looked at Gail's seat. "That's my seat," Denise said. "I always sit next to Gail."

"She's just going to sit here today," said Gail. "Her father asked me."

Denise made a face and looked around. "I guess I'll sit in the front," she said.

Mr. Jenkins was tall and thin with dark, curly hair. He welcomed the class to third grade. Then he welcomed Flory to Hillsdale.

"Are you getting settled in your new home?" he asked Flory. Flory still didn't feel Joe's house was her real home, but she nodded anyway.

"Well, good," said Mr. Jenkins. "We're glad to have you here."

Flory smiled. Mr. Jenkins seemed nice. Her first day wasn't bad, but Flory still missed her old school in Bay City. She kept wondering what Jenny and her other friends were doing. She decided to call Jenny as soon as she got home.

When Flory got on the bus after school, Gail and Denise were already sitting next to each other. Flory found a seat in the back of the bus.

Flory's mom met Flory and Nicky at the bus stop. "So how was your first day at school?" Flory's mom asked her.

"OK," said Flory. "Mr. Jenkins seems nice."

"Great!" her mom said.

At home, Nicky went outside to play with one of his friends from the neighborhood. Flory and her mom sat together in the kitchen. "Did you like riding a bus to school?" her mom asked.

Flory told her about Joe singing the ABC song as they walked to the bus. Flory rolled her eyes. "The kids in front of us were staring at him," Flory said.

Her mom laughed. "Oh you know, Joe. He was just kidding around." Flory used to think Joe was funny. Now, she wasn't so sure. It was a lot different living in the same house with him than just seeing him once in a while.

Flory asked her mom if she could call Jenny. When Jenny picked up the phone, Flory felt so happy. They talked about school and dance and a lot of other things, too. Flory missed going to dance class. Flory and Jenny wanted to be dancers when they grew up. Flory couldn't wait for Jenny to come visit.

Chapter 5

On Friday night, Flory's dad came to pick her up for the weekend. Since her mom and dad's divorce, Flory stayed with her dad every other weekend. When the doorbell rang, Flory ran to the door to see her dad.

Flory's dad hugged her. "*Mi hija bonita*—my beautiful daughter," he said.

"Don't forget to bring Flory back by six o'clock on Sunday," Flory's mom said.

Flory's dad nodded as he walked with Flory to his car. "Why are you bringing me back early?" Flory asked. "You don't bring me back until later on Sunday."

"Your mom said you're going to Joe's parents' house for dinner," Flory's dad said. "She asked me if I could bring you back a few hours earlier."

Flory sighed hard and wondered, *Why didn't Mom tell me we were going to Joe's parents' house?*

Flory had a good time at her dad's house. At least at her dad's house, everything was the same as usual.

On Monday, Flory's mom worked late at the department store. Joe was home after school.

After Flory finished her homework, Nicky asked her to play soccer with him. They went out front and started kicking the ball back and forth. Some of the other neighborhood kids came by and started to play. Gail was riding her bike and asked if she could play, too.

"Let's play boys versus girls," said Flory. They split into two teams—three boys and three girls. Gail was a pretty good soccer player.

A little while later, Joe came out onto the front porch. "Game over, soccer stars," he called out. "Nicky and Flory—it's time for dinner."

Flory and Nicky said goodbye to the other kids and came inside. After they washed up, they sat down to eat. Joe's lasagna tasted really good. And the garlic bread was crusty on the outside and soft on the inside—just the way Flory liked it.

"I made lasagna for your mom on one of our first dates," Joe told Flory. He winked at her. "I think that's the only reason she married me—she likes my cooking." Flory grinned.

Then, Joe turned to Nicky. "Are you ready for your soccer game tomorrow?" he asked. "Remember, Coach Sheila says you have to pass the ball to your teammates. You can't always kick the ball into the net yourself."

"I know," Nicky said. "Coach Sheila told me."

Chapter 6

Later, when Flory's mom came home from work, she hurried to see Flory. "Guess what?" she said excitedly. "I've signed you up for a ballet class at Hillsdale School of Dance! I spoke to Joe about it and the hours are good. On Tuesdays, Joe can take you, and on Thursdays, I can take you. Isn't that great?"

Flory frowned. "Mom, why didn't you ask me first?"

Flory's mom stared at her. "What do you mean?" she asked. "You love dance. You have been telling me how much you have missed it since we moved."

"But I didn't want to take ballet this year. I wanted to take jazz," Flory said. "Jenny is taking jazz, and she loves it. You didn't even talk to me about it—you and Joe are deciding everything for me!" Flory cried.

"I'm sorry, Florinda," her mom said. "This move is a big change for all of us. Joe and I are just trying to coordinate everyone's schedule along with our work hours, so we can be a family."

"Weren't we a family before?" Flory asked.

Flory's mom smiled and put her arm around Flory. "Yes, of course we were a family before." She hugged Flory. "I'm glad you told me how you feel," she said. "I've been so busy, I have forgotten how much we used to talk things over."

Chapter 7

The next day, Flory's mom picked up Nicky from soccer practice. Nicky came home with a scowl. "I don't like Coach Sheila anymore!" he told Joe.

"Why, what happened?" his father asked.

"She says I'm hogging the ball. She says I'm not passing to anyone," Nicky complained. "But I'm the one who scores the most!"

"When you were in kindergarten, just kicking the ball into the net was fun," said Joe. "But Coach Sheila now wants you to learn some real soccer skills."

"Soccer is a team sport," Flory added. "One person can't always have the ball."

"That's true," said Flory's mom. She looked at Flory. "A soccer team is almost like a family. Each person is an important part of the team."

Flory smiled. Maybe her mom really did understand.

On Friday night, Flory's mom and Joe talked about their plans for the weekend. They needed to do a lot of things around the house. Then they turned to Flory.

"How would you like to go shopping?" Flory's mom asked.

"For what?" Flory asked.

"Oh, to a paint store and to a home store," said Flory's mom. She grinned. "That way you can pick out just the color paint and blanket you would like for your bedroom."

A big smile spread across Flory's face. "Yes, I want to go shopping!" Flory exclaimed.

Chapter 8

On Saturday morning, Flory and her family went to a paint store. Flory didn't realize how many shades of blue there were. And there seemed to be 100 of them. Flory decided on a color called periwinkle. It looked like a combination of blue and purple.

Then they went to a bedding store. There were a lot of blankets and comforters. Flory went up and down the aisle, looking at all the blankets.

"How about this one?" asked Joe. He pointed to a blanket that had blue and yellow stripes with butterflies.

"Oooh, that's so pretty," said Flory.

Flory's mom looked at the blanket. "Yes, that really is pretty," she said. "That's a great choice, Flory."

The next day, they all painted Flory's room. Even Nicky helped. He got a lot of paint on him, almost as much as he got on the walls! Flory had fun watching the room change from pink to blue.

The periwinkle blue walls looked great. And she loved her new blanket and matching curtains.

Flory looked around her new bedroom. Joe's house was finally starting to feel like a home—her home.

Chapter 9

The next weekend, Jenny came to visit Flory for a sleepover. The two girls hugged each other at the door.

"Wait till you see my new room!" Flory exclaimed.

Jenny followed Flory up the stairs. Flory opened the bedroom door.

"Wow, your room looks great!" said Jenny.

"We all painted it. I painted it, too," Flory added.

Later on, the doorbell rang. Flory's mom called up the stairs to tell Flory that Gail was at the door.

"Tell her to come upstairs," Flory called to her mom.

Flory introduced Jenny to Gail. Flory had a great time with her friends that day. They played some games in her room and ate lunch together. After lunch, Flory happily said, "Let's go play in the backyard." Then she smiled. "*My* backyard."